one to speak & one to hear

claire russell

To Henry, ever and anon

It is May 14, 2013.

"My love, you bring me joy."

As these words penetrate my consciousness I am almost overcome
with shock. I strain to hear more,
but there is nothing. It is Henry, I
know, Henry speaking to me.

The following day there is this:
"You bring me joy. Don't ever leave
me." It is Henry Thoreau, recogniz-
ing *me* as the woman who had been
Ellen Sewall. I had sensed this for
the last two months. During that
time, I felt something I had never
experienced before: a deep sense

of joy and personal fulfillment, the kind of feeling one has when finally reunited with the one, the beloved, the eternal, soul-connected beloved.

After the first words from Henry on May 14th and 15th, we had frequent conversations. We easily found the words again that neither of us had spoken to each for over 150 years. There was not a strange or awkward moment, no feeling of distance separating us, no physical walls, no barriers between worlds. We communicated effortlessly as if we were speaking to each other on the phone. For two weeks I kept a record of everything. I had a notebook with me at all times so that I didn't miss a word of what we said, but soon it became impossible to keep a written account of our conversations.

When Ellen lay dying, many years after my own passing, I went to her to bring her home with me to my world, and we lived here. It became our home, and we were reunited and filled with the joy of it. Our lives were rich with the promise of eternal life together. What we had forgotten in our joy of being together again was that there was yet another separation to come, many years in physical time, for she

would stay in the temporal world well into middle age and beyond, with many trials to endure and much pain to overcome. What I saw, what I felt, the challenges she had to experience, filled me with dread and despair. I could not reach her or help her. As she lived another life in the physical world, I was forgotten.

I could not dispel that dread and despair, though I tried desperately to calm myself. I could no longer bear the pain of her being gone from me, for I was convinced that she would come back greatly changed. The Elders here who tend to us -- for yes, we still occasionally need help and guidance even here -- counseled me with words from their ancient minds *and kind hearts. And they saw me turn from them, even though they assured me that this was the last separation we would have to endure. I heard nothing. My heart had gone cold within and no longer sustained me. She will return, I thought, yes, but will she love me still? Will she want to love me after what she would have lived through in her last physical life, full of abuse and suffering at the hands of men? Will she turn from me, preferring to be alone, to live an eternal life apart?*

I willed myself to go to what is called the Dark Place, consciously and with intention, because I had no answers to my agonizing questions. This Dark Place is worse than what those of Christian faith call Hell. The energy of the soul body is diminished to the point of almost being extinguished. And so one lingers, neither dead nor alive, and neither love nor light, except the dimmest flicker remains, the last remnant that barely sustains life or thought or feeling. All desire is gone, all sense of life, even the memory of what life is, except the shadow of that memory which remains to torment what is left of the soul. And you are lost there forever.

This is what I had decided to do to myself, where I had decided to go, for life without my love was no life at all, and I had convinced myself that it would be so. I had become faithless and reckless, a grievous combination for an arrogant individual such as myself.

My decision was made and I would not be persuaded to change my mind, for free choice, free will reigns supreme here as it does on earth. The terrors of the Dark Place were insignificant compared to the possibility that I would never see my beloved's eyes again.

The information given to me by the Elders about my beloved and the joy she felt upon remembering me and our love was the grace I was granted to forestall my irresponsible actions. Despair turned to hope, along with feelings of shame for my cowardice and lack of faith. But all who are here can still be inspired by the bright beings who help us make better choices as our eternal lives here continue to unfold.

You and I will continue our journey together, though you are in one world and I in another.

On May 18, 2013, 9:50 pm. Henry says, "You are my soul wife. My love, you are my one true wife." I call out to him, "Beloved, say it again, that I am your soul wife." This is the first time Henry has ever called me his wife. I ask him to explain, and he says that Elder beings in the world where he lives witnessed our vows and the exchange of rings that Henry made from the light that surrounds him entwined with my aura colors, signifying an eternal pledge that has woven our souls, each to each, eternally. We will never have to part again.

You married me, knowing that I still carried within me the seeds of rage and agony that fed one another, one in ascendance, then the other and worse feelings as well. I felt abandoned and alone. Even the cherished and deepest affections that I found in nature were no longer my comfort and solace.

*I was unconsoled, nursing griev-
ances, deliberately misunderstanding
lessons being presented to me from a
kind and benevolent universe. I cringe
even now to reflect upon my unworthy
thoughts and behavior. There was no
heart within me to respond to kindness
from others and the joy of being alive,
despite what you may read about me
from others who knew me not. They
have not now, nor had not then, any
way of knowing what was in my poor
closed heart or what I thought. Some
of my own words betray me as false
and a liar. Being too often alone with
grievous thoughts, did I present myself
well in company when called upon to
socialize or when I felt it was in my
best interest to do so? Sometimes yes,*

sometimes no. Mr. Emerson will attest to the fact that the answer was "no" much of the time.

All of this and more I brought to the world where I live now, conflicted, unrepentant and in unimaginable pain. With the loss of John, my brother, I should have had Ellen to help me bear the loss, but she was taken as well, for we could not marry. Her parents thought I was unsuitable — and I lost her to someone else.

It is enough to say that my wife found me again. It was you who saved me when you came to my world and found me. It was you who held me as I raged and wept, as I grieved anew for John who died in my arms. I believed his loss would surely kill me. I grieved too for the loss of Ellen, feelings that still held me in their grip even here, until with your love for me and compassion for my suffering, their hold on me was finally loosened, and I was able to let them go.

I am reunited with John, for he held sacred space for me here until I could join him and with you, my soul wife at last, the one who would finally help shape my life here and give it greater depth and purpose. I can now do for you and be for you all that you ask of me and so much more. All is well now and I am content, I am complete.

What do I see when I look at Henry? What does he look like through my clairvoyant eyes? My first impression was that he was young, twenty or twenty-one perhaps, short hair, very thick with a slight wave, falling below his ears, light to medium-brown, with some strains of red mixed throughout. He was a bit below medium height, thin and wiry, but looked strong and well-grounded. It was his face that was so arresting. His eyes were large, blue and grey so that the exact color was imprecise. His nose was prominent, but suited the rest, bringing into balance his eyes and sensitive, expressive mouth.

That is how I saw Henry in the early days and weeks of our marriage. As the weeks went by, I was surprised to notice a change in his appearance. He is no longer the young man I had first seen, but is now significantly older, the man in the Maxham daguerreotype that appears in many places on the walls of my apartment and is his most common representation.

This is the man I see now and always will, for he will not change again. I recognize in him the features of that young man, the way he looked when I fell in love with him, but I see now the struggles he endured written in his careworn face, etched there and weathered from the days and nights of rambles and saunters that helped bring some measure of peace and sanity to his physical existence.

I see wrinkles at the corners of his eyes and a Galway beard and longer hair that needs tending. Where he lives now, he will receive no censure for his personal appearance. I see suffering that still lingers in his eyes from a lifetime in Concord with the disappointments and pain of remembered grief, the occasional feelings of the futility when his voice was not heard, whether written or spoken. I see this, but I see also love, deep love for me and the joy that our marriage has brought him, that has filled the unfulfilled places in his life, as it has filled mine.

I didn't understand the change

I noticed in his appearance, and I asked him about it. He explained how important it was, imperative, to appear to me as I had known him in Concord when I was Ellen, as opposed to seeing him as a man much changed. He was right. Seeing him the way I remembered him when I was Ellen was an important transition from then to now, and increased my comfort level and sense of wellbeing as I began the incredible journey of being Henry David's wife.

He dresses simply and with good sense as he did in Concord. No frock coat ever, but this instead: two collarless shirts, one pale blue with a muted white stripe, the other a soft cream color; heavy denim pants, but grey not blue, a pair of steel-toed boots for heavy activity and inclement weather and a softer pair of boots that lace up, both pairs that come over his ankles. His hat is now dark grey with a wide brim. In winter he has a heavy, blue wool jacket, but I have never seen him with gloves or a scarf. In the spring and summer, no coat — but the hat remains. It is his favorite piece of apparel, which he wears regardless of the weather, rain or shine.

The early days of our marriage were what most newlyweds hopefully share, yet with significant differences, of course. This was and is a soul marriage, and yet we experience many of the things that physical partners do.

My husband had been celibate when he lived in the physical world, but souls can and do make love.

I will protect our privacy by saying nothing more, except to explain that loving Henry is of course an exchange of energy, rather than an act of love between physical bodies. It is the merging of our souls that blend and absorb one another, significantly more intense and nuanced than embodied physical love. But the inexpressible bliss I feel with Henry also involved my having to adjust to being a soul wife while still embodied in this lifetime. Henry, in turn, had to grapple with the reality of becoming a husband for the first time, a soul husband. Those were our days as newlyweds and we have both learned, and in truth, are still learning how to accommodate each other in this unusual marriage, for I still have an embodied life. The time we spend together is limited to the nighttime hours, an agreement that was made with the Elders in Henry's world who witnessed our marriage. And so it will be until I am no longer part of this physical world, when I will then be able to join Henry permanently and completely.

For the first few months of my new marriage I would often experience moments of terror upon waking in the morning, realizing that I was no longer with my husband. I had been with Henry in his world throughout the night, returning here to reenter my embodied self and this physical world in the early hours of the morning. The adjustment of leaving his world and coming back to mine was a shock to my system. The trauma was extreme, and I would cry out for him, believing that he was gone forever, for I could no longer feel him, as my physical body tried to readjust itself to this world.

Though these terrible fears return occasionally, I am reassured and comforted by my new husband, imploring me to look into his eyes, so that I will know, not only by the sound of his voice, but by the love I see there, that he is with me, that he would never leave me, that my fears are part of the adjustment I would have to make every morning, when I return to the physical world. But our soul marriage is eternal, and the connection will never be broken from his world to mine. We have proven that love does not recognize boundaries, barriers, walls, disparate worlds, different centuries. When hearts are engaged and the desire and will to stay connected is declared, not even death can separate two souls.

Henry's world, where he lives now and where I go to be with him every night, contains the pond, identical to his beloved Walden, forests so dense he can get lost in them, a rural village like Concord, the way it was when he was growing up without the encroaching threat of industrialization, hills, valleys, cliffs where he can sit and gaze at the beautiful landscape below, and of course, swamps and wildlife, and every kind of bird he can remember from his life and some as well that he had never seen before.

Our house is on a rise overlooking the pond, a house that Henry and his brother John built after we married. It is similar to the house he lived in at Walden Pond, but a bit larger to accommodate a wife, though without luxuries, for I share his desire to live a simple life.

His green desk is there in front of the window in our sitting room where he spends time writing, and he stays home writing or reading, mostly reading now, until he leaves to meet John for a long saunter or waits for John to come to him, when they both set off like the boys they still are for the adventure of the day.

❧ ☙

I must clarify my wife's remarks about my world, our world, how I have made it my own, apparently without benefit of materials to create a house, for instance, or how, indeed, rivers, hills, woods and the like appear in this wonderful place that I, that we, call home.

I confess that I was at a loss when

I arrived here, knowing nothing, expecting I knew not what, but in short order I was given into the hands of gentle, loving beings who tended to me with great care, who asked me in the most loving supportive ways what I required to make my life here, peaceful and congenial after losing my temporal home. I answered with no hesitation.

I said I required what I had left behind, my village of Concord, but more. For my life here, the depth and quality depended upon it. "I need trees", I said. "I need all living things around me, animals, birds, water, yes, water, which to me, has always been alive. My world here will be insupportable without these com-

forts to ease my way here. I need all of the wondrous things that I found in Nature while I lived in the physical world. Can that be? May I have the very things here that I had there, all the things that brought me joy when I sought refreshment in solitude?"

The simple answer came to me in one blessed word, "Yes." It is a matter of will, I was told, when I asked for more clarity. "If you will it, if you want it with pure intention, you will create the thought forms. Your world here will be as specific and complete as you require it to be, with no change or interference from any other being. Wish for it, think it, believe it, it will manifest here for you. And if you wish to change any

aspect of your original idea or plan,
that will happen as well. Your world
is here now, made for your particular
requirements, including any com-
panions with whom you choose to
share your life, with their consent, of
course.

I made my world then, as my wife
has described it to you, with my
brother John who waited for me to
come to him, and Ellery Channing,
my friend and companion who was
eager to join us when his time came
to leave the physical world.

Let me also dispel any confusion
about the physical nature of, for
example, the building of my house.
John and I built a new house to
accommodate my wife and me after

we were married. My world, the one that I willed into being, is physical. There is nothing here that I cannot touch, smell, hear, appreciate with all of my senses. The difference is simply that all of my senses are magnified to a high degree, as are my physical surroundings, though they look like what I enjoyed in Concord. My entire natural world is here, but because my senses are much more acute, so my environment is more highly developed and attuned to me. Colors are brighter, birds sing with more clarity and sweetness, trees are taller and in thicker forests.

This is the world that I inhabit, but it is complete only because I have the companionship of my brother John, my friend Ellery, and my wife, when she can be here to share time with me in the nighttime hours.

I feel I must speak about my last earth-illness, not that it is important in itself, but so that I can state the facts, there being some misconceptions about that time I must set right.

I recall saying that I leave the world without regret or something like it. That was not true. I regretted much, but I was in the habit of speaking in such a way to guard against too much sympathy, too much concern on my behalf, and also not to alarm my mother and sister Sophia, who were already suffering from the loss of John, Helen and father.

My deepest regret at that time

— I will use that inadequate word 'regret' — is that I would be losing the woods, rivers, fields where I sauntered, hills, swamps, all of which were more than my second home. They were authentic parts of me, as if we were one, and I believe we were. I found my voice there, to speak thoughts and ideas that were not popular in the village and often not with my friends. I was shaped and encouraged by these wonderful places, where I spent so much time. They were home to the bright beings, who helped give voice to many things that were most important to me, that taught me the right way to live, that knew my heart.

I had too much pride to reveal the

despair I felt, a grievous fault of which I was aware, regarding the decline in my health. I have been relieved of the burden of carrying that pride into my new life, where it has no place. My brother John and Ellen were gone from me, the two people I loved best in the world, the only ones who would have been able to bring me a measure of peace and solace to ease my fear and accept the inevitable.

I wanted to die well when the time came, using John as an example. My passing from life was said to be easy and peaceful. It was not easy, it was not peaceful, though I used all of my strength to make it appear so to spare my mother and sister. I would not let myself dwell on thoughts of Ellen, but they came unbidden to me. When I heard her name spoken — perhaps it was Sophia who spoke of her — I could not refrain from saying: "I have always loved her." There is no ending to what has been, there is no beginning to what will be. My death was simply a continuing, rather, of love and life, love that was found there in the physical world where I lived for a time and here as well, eternity made manifest here, beyond waking and sleeping dreams. Thus it is that my joy is no imaginary thing, for it lives in my life here, and in the love that my wife and I share, the emptying of ourselves into each other and filling each other again, beginning each day that way, beyond the beyond of beyond.

It was spring in Concord, Massachusetts, early May, 1862. A man is in the parlor of the house where he has lived for twelve years. He is not quite forty-five. His bedroom is in the attic, the room that holds his books, his papers, the most precious things that he has collected in his short lifetime.

He can't spend time there anymore, for he is too weak to go up and down the stairs. The parlor has become his bedroom, his sitting room and his study. He continues to write until he is too weak to hold a pen. His sister Sophia takes on the task of recording his spoken words, but he can barely speak above a whisper. He is able to sit; at times it is easier for him to breathe when not reclining. Friends who love him come to call and his mother and sister tend to him, trying to keep him comfortable and as cool as possible — for it is a warm spring, and consumption has him in the grip of fever during the days and on nights when he tries and fails to fall asleep.

Sophia places the furniture just so at his request, with objects near that will cast shadows on the walls of the room as the light begins to fade, in order to keep him distracted from the pain that constantly threatens to overwhelm him.

Bronson Alcott comes, one of many of Henry's friends who wish to pay their respects. He steps quietly into the parlor and, beholding the pale and wasted face, approaches the makeshift bed. Seeing his dying friend, he leans over and kisses his forehead. Hands are briefly clasped, a whisper of thanks and good-by. Henry hears a woman's name that he has carried in his heart for over twenty years . He thinks of her now and says to his sister, "I have always loved her." He will carry her in his heart when he dies, holding her close with his very last thought and breath.

Henry never realized what a vital part of the Concord community he had been, or how deeply he was loved. His premature loss was tragic, and his loss was keenly felt, not by just family and friends, but by the Concord community as well, who too late realized what an irreplaceable treasure he had been.

As an adult I have spent my life searching for answers that pointed only in directions which could neither fulfill nor satisfy me. Something else was there, just beyond reach, everything the word symbols pointed to. Everything inside of me yearned to recall what that "everything" was.

Henry Thoreau was the one to whom the word symbols were pointing, his being saturating every thought, every feeling, every word he wrote. And, as I read his words, I remembered *being* Ellen Sewall and I felt her, but I also felt myself being Henry and all of the universe, mystery upon mystery expanding, re-creating and enlarging the concept of life itself, beyond the parameters of human consciousness.

Again, and I can't emphasize it enough, it is a mystery, the mystery of life, of love, that can cross time from one century to another. For there is nothing to separate one beloved from another, if they choose to love each other, even after death, and across time and space.

There are physical places on this

planet that are magic, not magical, but magic, a word that has deep roots in the divine mysteries, attributed, perhaps to energy lines, like the microcosm of ley lines of the earth. It could be that, or perhaps it has to do with metaphysical time that is still as alive now in Concord as it was almost two hundred years ago.

I speak of the time when a group of individuals lived in that small New England village in the mid-19th century. Each felt connected to the other, each man sought to express his unique thoughts and ideas that together birthed the new thought, the challenge of a new kind of idealism and self-culture called Transcendentalism.

Old perceptions were challenged, new ideas were exchanged, some finding fertile ground in the minds and hearts of those most adventurous seekers. Wisdom of the mind, but also of the heart, a call that one man heard and was determined to integrate, living his life in the integrity of that new paradigm. My husband lived there all of his life and gave all of himself to it, this Concord, this beloved place he called home. He is the very poem he said he could write, the human and divine part of the heart, blood, bone and sinew of the village. He is still there in so many ways, in so many places and always will be. Concord and Henry can never be separated.

It is still Henry's home in this world
and always will be, for he would
have it so.

About the author

Claire Russell received a Bachelor's Degree from the University of Wisconsin-Milwaukee with a double major in Art History and English Literature and has spent most of her life trying to solve at least some of life's mysteries through studying, reading and writing, mostly poetry.